This edition first published in
Great Britain by
Pelham Books Ltd
44 Bedford Square
London WC1B 3DP
1976

Reprinted 1985

First published in Denmark by
Gyldendalske Boghandel in 1976
as *Tommeliden*

Illustrations Copyright
© 1976 Svend Otto S.
English Translation Copyright
© 1976 Pelham Books Ltd

ISBN 0 7207 0914 8

Printed in Denmark

Filmset by Spectrum Typesetting Ltd.

GRIMM # Tom Thumb

Translated by Anthea Bell

Illustrated by Svend Otto S.

Pelham Books

Once upon a time there was a poor countryman, and he was sitting by his fireside one evening poking the fire, while his wife sat and span. "How sad I am that we have no children!" said he. "This place is so quiet, and other people's houses are all so lively and merry!"

"Yes," said his wife, sighing, "if only we had a child, just one, however small, even a child no bigger than my thumb, then I'd be happy, and we would love it dearly!"

Well, seven months later it so happened that she did have a child, a little boy who was perfectly formed in every way, but no bigger than a man's thumb.

So the countryman and his wife said, "Well, we have what we wanted, and he is our own dear child." And because the boy was so small, they called him Tom Thumb.

They gave him plenty to eat, but he never grew any bigger; he stayed as small as the day he was born. However, he had a pair of quick bright eyes. Soon he proved to be a clever, nimble boy, and whatever he set out to do, he did it well.

One day his father was going off to the forest to chop some wood, and he said, half to himself, "I wish I had someone to follow me with the cart."

"Oh, don't you worry, Father," said Tom Thumb. "I'll bring the cart to the forest for you whenever you need it."

That made his father laugh. "How could you do that?" he asked. "You're far too small to drive a horse and cart!"

"Never mind that, Father. If Mother will harness up the horse, I'll sit in his ear and tell him which way to go."

"Very well," said his father. "There's no harm in trying."

So when the time came, Tom Thumb's mother harnessed up the horse, lifted Tom Thumb up, and he sat in the horse's ear and called out which way they were to go. "Gee up!" he shouted. All went well; Tom Thumb might have been driving a horse and cart all his life, and they took the right path to the forest. But just as the cart was turning a corner, and Tom Thumb was calling, "Whoa there!" two strangers came by.

"Good Heavens!" said one of them. "Whatever is that? I can see a cart going along the road, and I can hear a driver calling out to the horse, yet there isn't any driver to be seen!"

"There's something funny about it, sure enough," agreed the other man. "Let's follow and see where the cart is going."

The cart went on, right into the forest, to the place where Tom Thumb's father was chopping wood. When Tom Thumb saw his father, he called out, "You see, Father? Here I am, and here's the cart too! Lift me down now."

His father held the horse with his left hand, took Tom Thumb out of the horse's ear with his right hand, and Tom Thumb sat down on a blade of grass, very pleased with himself.

When the two strangers caught sight of Tom Thumb, they were so surprised, they could not speak. But then one of them drew the other aside. "Listen, that little fellow might make our fortunes!" said he. "We could put him on show in some big city, and make people pay to see him. Let's buy him!"

So they went up to Tom Thumb's father and said, "Will you sell us that little fellow? We'll take good care of him."

"Oh, no," said the father. "I can't do that; he's the apple of my eye, and I wouldn't part with him for all the gold in the world!"

However, when Tom Thumb heard this bargaining, he climbed the folds of his father's coat, got up on his shoulder, and whispered in his ear, "Go on, Father, sell me! I'll soon come home again." So his father sold him to the two strangers for a great deal of money.

"Now, where would you like to sit?" asked one of the men.

"Oh, just put me on the brim of your hat," said Tom Thumb. "I can walk up and down there and look at the view. I won't fall off."

So they did as he asked, and when Tom Thumb had said goodbye to his father they all three set off together.

On they went, till twilight began to fall, and the little boy said, "Put me down, please. It's urgent!"

"No, you just stay where you are," said the man on whose head he was standing. "Nothing you do will bother me; I've had bird droppings on this hat before now!"

"No, no!" said Tom Thumb. "I know what's right and proper. Quick, do put me down!"

So the man took off his hat and put the little boy down in a field by the wayside. Tom Thumb scurried about among the clods of earth for a moment or so, and then, spotting a mousehole, he crawled inside it.

"Goodbye, gentlemen!" said he. "You can go off home without me!"

And he laughed and laughed. They came and poked sticks down the mousehole, and that did them no good; Tom Thumb just crept further in, and as it was soon quite dark they had to go home empty-handed, in a very bad temper.

When Tom Thumb was sure they had gone, he crept out of the mousehole again. "Crossing a field like this in the dark is dangerous," he thought. "I could easily break a leg, or my neck." But luckily he came upon an empty snail-shell. "That's a good thing!" he said. "I can spend the night quite safely here." And he went inside.

Quite soon, just as he was dropping off to sleep, he heard two men walking by.

"Now," one of them was saying to the other, "how shall we set about stealing that rich minister's money and his silver?"

Tom Thumb spoke up. "I can tell you how!" said he.

"What was that?" asked the thief, in alarm. "I'm sure I heard a voice!"

They stopped and listened, and Tom Thumb spoke up again. "Take me with you, and I'll help you."

"But where are you?"

"Just look down on the ground here, and you'll find where my voice is coming from," said Tom Thumb.

So at last the thieves found him and picked him up. "Well, little fellow, and how can you help us?" they asked.

"Why," said Tom Thumb, "I can creep through the iron bars across the window of the minister's room and hand you out the things you want."

"Very well," they said, "let's try it!"

When they came to the house, Tom Thumb crept into the minister's room, but once inside he shouted at the top of his voice, "Do you want everything that's here?"

The thieves were scared. "Hush!" they said. "Keep your voice down, or you'll wake the household!"

But Tom Thumb pretended not to understand them, and he shouted out again, "What do you want? Do you want everything that's here?"

Now the maidservant sleeping in the next room heard him, and she sat up in bed and listened. The thieves had run a little way off in their fright, but at last they plucked up courage again. "The little fellow's only teasing us," they thought, so they came back and whispered, "Come along, now, no more joking! Just pass the stuff out!"

Then Tom Thumb shouted again, as loud as ever he could:
"Here, just put your hands in through the bars, and you can have it all!"

The maidservant, who was listening, heard him quite clearly, and she jumped out of bed and stumbled in through the door. The thieves ran away; they ran and ran as if the Devil himself were after them. Since the maidservant could not see anything, she went to fetch a light, and when she came back Tom Thumb managed to get out of the house without being noticed, and into the barn. As for the maidservant, when she had searched the whole room and still found nothing, at last she went back to bed, thinking she must have been dreaming with her eyes open.

Tom Thumb climbed into a heap of hay and found a good place to sleep; he decided to spend the night there and then go home to his parents. But there were more adventures in store for him!

When day dawned, the maidservant got up to go and feed the animals. The first place she went to was the barn, where she picked up an armful of hay, and it happened to be the hay where Tom Thumb was sleeping. Indeed, he was so fast asleep that he never noticed anything, and he didn't wake up until he was right inside the cow's mouth, along with some of the hay.

"Dear me!" he cried. "However did I get into this mill?" Soon, however, he realized where he was. He had to be very careful to avoid the cow's teeth, which might have chewed him up any moment, and then down he slid into her stomach.

"They forgot the windows when they built this room," said he. "The sun can't shine in, and there isn't any lamp either!" He didn't like the place at all, and even worse, more and more hay kept coming in at the door, so that soon there was hardly any space left. At last he felt so frightened that he called out, as loud as he could, "No more hay, please! No more hay, please!"

The maidservant was just milking the cow when she heard someone speak, though she could not see him, and it was the very same voice she had heard the night before.

She was so frightened that she tumbled off her stool and spilled the bucket of milk. Off she ran to her master, as fast as she could go.

"Oh, sir!" she cried. "Our cow is talking!"

"Nonsense! You must be out of your mind!" said the minister. However, he went off to the cowshed himself to see what was going on.

No sooner did he set foot inside the shed than Tom Thumb started shouting again. "No more hay, please! No more hay, please!"

This frightened the minister, too. He thought his cow must be possessed by some evil demon, and he gave orders for her to be killed. So the cow was slaughtered, and her stomach, with Tom Thumb still inside it, was thrown on the dung heap. Tom Thumb had a hard job of it working his way out, but at last he made enough room to struggle free. However, just as he was about to pop his head out . . .

. . . he had another piece of bad luck. A hungry wolf came prowling by and swallowed the cow's stomach whole, in a single gulp. But Tom Thumb did not lose heart. "Perhaps this wolf will listen to me," he thought, and he called out from inside the wolf, "Dear Mr. Wolf, I can tell you where to find delicious things to eat!"

"Can you, indeed?" asked the wolf. "Where?"

"In a house I know. You must get in through the drain in the wall, and then you'll see all the cakes and bacon and sausages you can eat." And Tom Thumb told the wolf the way to his father's house.

The wolf wasn't wasting any time. That very night he got into the larder through the drain, and ate as much as he wanted. When he had had enough, he tried to get out again, but by now he was so fat that he could not leave the same way as he had come. That was what Tom Thumb had been hoping for, and now he began making a lot of noise inside the wolf, shouting and yelling at the top of his voice.

"Be quiet, can't you?" said the wolf. "You'll wake the household!"

"What if I do?" said Tom Thumb. "You've had your feast, now it's my turn for a bit of fun!"

And he began shouting at the top of his voice again.

At last the noise woke his father and mother. They came running to the larder and looked in through a crack in the door. When they saw a wolf inside they hurried off — his father to get his axe and his mother to fetch the scythe.

"Now, you stand back," said the man to his wife, as they came back to the larder. "I shall hit him with the axe, and if that doesn't kill him then you must cut his body open."

Tom Thumb, hearing his father's voice, called out, "Here I am, Father! I'm inside the wolf!"

"Thank heavens!" cried his father joyfully. "Our own dear child is home again!"

And he told his wife to put down the scythe for fear of hurting Tom Thumb. Then he swung his axe, and gave the wolf such a mighty blow that he fell down dead. Tom Thumb's mother and father fetched a knife and a pair of scissors, cut open the wolf's body and found their little boy.

"Dear me, we've been so worried about you!" said his father.

"Oh, Father, I've had so many adventures! How glad I am to breathe fresh air again!"

"But where have you been all this time?"

"I've been down a mousehole, Father, in the stomach of a cow, and in the wolf's belly, and now I'm back home!"

"And we'll never sell you again, not for all the money in the world!" said his parents, hugging and kissing their own dear little Tom Thumb. They gave him something to eat and something to drink, and they had new clothes made for him, because his old ones were ruined after all his adventures.

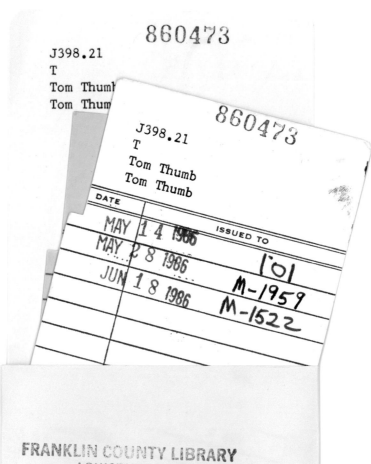